Other titles in the That's Nat Series

Natalie

and the Downside-Up Birthday

Dandi Daley Mackall

For Lawson Pento — Happy Birthday!

ZONDERKIDZ

Natalie and the Downside-Up Birthday
Copyright © 2009 by Dandi Daley Mackall
Illustrations © 2009 by Lys Blakeslee

Requests for information should be addressed to:
Zonderkidz, 3900 Sparks Dr. SE, Grand Rapids, Michigan 49546

Library of Congress Cataloging-in-Publication Data:
Mackall, Dandi Daley.
  Natalie and the downside-up birthday / by Dandi Daley Mackall.
     p. cm. — (That's Nat!)
  Summary: Five-year-old Natalie is so excited about her birthday parties—a kindergarten
version and a home party too—until she discovers she has a "birthday buddy," the not-so-
nice Sasha.
  ISBN 978-0-310-71569-6 (softcover)
[1. Birthdays—Fiction. 2. Parties—Fiction. 3. Sharing—Fiction. 4. Christian life—Fiction. 5.
Kindergarten—Fiction. 6. Schools—Fiction.] I. Title.
  PZ7.M1905Nad 2009
  [Fic]—dc22   2008049737

Editor: Betsy Flikkema
Art direction and design: Merit Alderink

Printed in the United States of America

Table of Contents

Chapter 1

The Secret Surprise

My name is Natalie 24, and I've got a secret surprise.

That secret surprise is about my name. *Hint, hint.* 'Cause in case you didn't notice, my name is also a number. Twenty-four. My very favoritest number in the whole wide world.

My bestest friends and parents can call me "Nat 24," since that is my nickname, which is also my nick-number.

But that's not the secret surprise.

My mom and dad get very aggravated at me when I spill out their secrets and surprises. *Aggravated* is what other moms and dads call "mad."

So I will just give you another *hint, hint*. On account of a hint is not really telling the secret or spoiling the surprise.

Here is another *hint*. Take my favorite number, 24, and pull those numbers apart, and you get a 2 and a 4. And that 2 can stand for Month Number Two, which goes by the name of February. And 4 can stand for Day Number Four. So that makes February 4. Get it?

February 4 is coming tomorrow. That's what.

And that's a huge *hint* for you about the secret surprise.

Plus also, here are some more *hints*, in case you're having a bad day or maybe not paying good attention:

I am getting a chocolate cake with chocolate frosting.

That chocolate cake will have a picture of a white cat named Percy on top of it.

There will be candles on there too. Six candles. *Hint, hint*.

There will be presents! For *me*!

I am five and a half years old today. But tomorrow, on February 4, I won't be that anymore or ever again, which is a tiny bit sad, only not so much. Tomorrow, I will be six! Like Peter and Chase and some other kids in my kindergarten.

I love secret surprises and especially this one.

A secret is something you know and other people don't.

A surprise is something coming that you don't know about or don't know when it's coming.

So if you think about it, maybe this isn't a secret since I know it already and so do a bunch of people.

Plus also, maybe this is not a surprise. We know when it is coming. Tomorrow. February 4.

So maybe telling this isn't like spilling out a secret surprise that will make your mom and dad aggravated at you.

'Sides, I can't stand keeping this secret any longer. This secret feels like a balloon inside of my head getting bigger and bigger until it pops out of my mouth.

Ready?

Here is the secret surprise that may not be a secret surprise after all:

I am going to have a birthday!

Tomorrow!

Plus also, a big fat birthday party. That's what.

Only it's kind of a secret surprise. So don't tell anybody.

Chapter 2

Invites

I walk up the school sidewalk with my bestest friend
who is a girl, Laurie. This is a happy thing and kind
of a surprise on account of I didn't know when
Laurie would get here. Her mom drives her, and my
mom drives me. And my mom drives much faster
than Laurie's mom. So I am usually here first and
have to wait for Laurie.

Only, *surprise!* Not today.

"I got your birthday party invitation!" Laurie
shouts to me, even though I am right here by her.

"You did?" I ask. Only I know she did. My
bestest friend, Laurie, is a truther and not a liar.

Plus also, I know she's coming to my birthday
party. We have talked very much about this party.

My party is going to happen on Saturday instead
of on my real birthday that's on Friday, which is
tomorrow. And that can get mixed up in your head if
you let it.

"I *loved* your invitation!" Laurie says.

"I picked them out myself," I tell her. This is a
true thing. I picked an invitation with a cake 'cause
I will have one of those cakes at my party.

Laurie and I hold hands and skip up the sidewalk.

"Don't step on that crack," Laurie warns. "Step on a crack, break your mother's back."

I jump over that crack. I love my mother's back.

Laurie and I are both wearing purple gloves. We love that purpley color. We are holding our lunch boxes in our outside hands and holding each other's hands with our inside hands.

We get to the front school step, when somebody whizzes right in between us. That somebody crashes into our arms and breaks our hand-holding. That someone is Sasha.

"Ouch!" Laurie cries. She drops her lunch box and has to pick it up.

"Sasha!" I yell. "That wasn't nice."

11

Sasha doesn't slow down or turn around or say sorry. She runs right into our classroom. This is how she gets her nickname, "Sasha-the-Not-So-Nice." She is best friends with "Peter-the-Not-So-Great."

Laurie and I tippytoe up the hall together, even though we don't have to. I stop us before we go in. "Laurie," I say, "do you think there are too many days in this week?"

"I think there's the regular amount of days, Nat," Laurie answers. "This is Thursday, and tomorrow is Friday, our last school day this week."

I know this week is taking longer than any other kindergarten week. It has been going to be my birthday forever. "Do you think there are more hours in the kindergarten days this week?" I ask Laurie.

Laurie folds in her lips and scrunches up her nose, 'cause that's how she does thinking. "You know, I think you're right, Nat. Yesterday's kindergarten went on and on and on."

I smile at Laurie 'cause I know she just agreed with me because she's my best friend. And that's a nice thing.

Farah runs up to us when we're hanging up our coats and putting our lunch boxes and packs in our cubbies. She has gorgeous hair that she can sit on. "I got your invitation," she whispers.

She glances at Sasha, who is hanging up a beautiful purple coat in her cubby. I have never seen this coat before. I have trouble stopping staring. I would very much love a purple coat exactly like that. Only different.

"You don't have to whisper," I tell Farah. "My mom made me invite everybody in the whole class—even Peter and even Sasha—so nobody would feel bad."

Farah grins. "You have a nice mother, Natalie."

"Thank you, Farah," I say. "So do you." I haven't met her mother, but she must be nice like Farah. I'm thinking Farah should call me Nat, like Laurie does. But before I can tell her so, Bethany dashes over to us, grabs Farah's elbow, and runs off.

I whisper to Laurie, "My mom is bringing cupcakes tomorrow for a classroom party."

"Cool!" Laurie says. "What kind of cupcakes?"

"We still have to make them, but they will be very chocolate," I tell her. "Granny and I are cooking the cupcakes tonight, and she loves chocolate. As soon as school's over, Mommy and I are going to the grocery store to get the 'gredients that go into cupcakes. Like chocolate. And icing. And maybe sprinkles."

"I love the grocery store," Laurie says. "Unless Mom has a list or she brings Brianna with us."

Brianna is one of Laurie's older sisters. And she is the bossy, gripey one.

"Let's go see Ham," Laurie says. She pulls me with her to the cage of our classroom pet.

Inside that cage is our hamster, who goes by the name of Ham the Hamster.

I stare in at Ham's big eyes and funny nose. But I don't put my face too close to the cage. This is one of the gazillion rules we have in this kindergarten place.

"Did you tell Ham a joke yet?" asks Jason. Jason is my bestest friend who is a boy. And that's not the same thing as a boyfriend. He's been chasing kids around the room, but he stops at Ham's cage and waits for me to answer his question.

"Not yet."

I started telling Ham jokes the second day of kindergarten. Now I do it every kindergarten morning. I am a very good joke-teller. This is 'cause

I have practice telling my cat, Percy, cat jokes. And sometimes dog jokes.

"Okay. How come the hamster crossed the road?" I ask Ham. I have a gazillion of these crossing-the-road jokes.

Ham doesn't answer. He never answers. And

that is a good thing. It gives me time to think of the joke answer.

I am thinking of a very funny answer to this joke. Like, *Why did the hamster cross the road? Because Sasha was on this side*.

Only I won't say this answer on account of Jesus wouldn't, not even if it was a very funny answer and people laughed, and Jesus loved people laughing. He wouldn't say mean things, even just to make people laugh. I have a bracelet with letters that proves it and reminds me to do what Jesus would do. Even though I don't have this bracelet on today because it's not purple, I remember anyway.

"So what's the end of the joke?" Peter-the-Not-So-Great demands.

Instead of using the Sasha answer, I answer, "Because its bestest friend, who goes by the name of Laurie Hamster, is on the other side already. That's what."

Laurie laughs her head off.

Jason makes car engine noises. Then he takes off running. "I'm crossing the road!" he screams.

Farah giggles.

Sasha makes a frowny face and says, "I don't get it."

Peter makes a frowny face and says, "That's not funny."

This turns Laurie and me into giggle boxes.

I am having a very fun time. And it's not even my birthday.

Yet!

Chapter 3

Waiting on 'Nouncements

School goes on pretty much like regular. Only very much longer than regular. This might could be on account of I am waiting for our teacher to make a 'nouncement about how tomorrow is February 4, and we will have a birthday party for me with cupcakes.

I know this is what happens. Other kids in my very own classroom already had their birthdays. And we got 'nouncements about it and mostly cupcakes. Miss Hines makes the 'nouncement a day ahead of time so we can be excited about it all night.

But we are almost at the end of the day. And Miss Hines still hasn't made the birthday 'nouncement. My stomach is starting to feel twitchy in a not-good way.

Like, what if the kindergarten birthday 'nouncement rule changed? And there can't be any more birthday cupcakes in the classroom?

Or, what if Miss Hines forgot that part about the 'nouncements?

Or, maybe she doesn't know that tomorrow is

Month Number Two and Day Number Four.

Or, what if—

"Class," Miss Hines says in her big voice, "please be quiet. I have an announcement."

I look two rows over to where my bestest friend, Laurie, is sitting. She is all smiley-faced back at me. Laurie knows about 'nouncements.

"Tomorrow," Miss Hines goes on, "we're getting a special treat. A birthday treat."

"Yea!" Jason yells.

Other kids shout too. They don't raise their hands, and they still don't get in trouble.

"Not only are we getting a classroom birthday party tomorrow," Miss Hines continues, "we're getting two birthday parties."

Jason and other kids yell, "Yippee!" and "Cool, dude!" and "Woo-hoo!"

Only not me.

Two birthdays?

I raise my hand, like the rule is. Only I don't wait for Miss Hines to call on me 'cause I can't wait. "Miss Hines, I'm only having one birthday," I tell her.

Miss Hines smiles. "I know, Natalie. But you have a birthday buddy in our classroom."

This is new news to me. It feels like bad news. Two four is *my* birthday. I never thought about sharing it. "Are you for certain sure somebody else in here has a birthday on February four?" I ask our teacher.

"Well, not exactly," she admits.

My heart slows down its pounding. My stomach stops twitching.

"But," Miss Hines continues, "someone else in our class has a birthday on February the fifth, the day after yours."

I am feeling way much better not sharing my birthday. "Then we're *not* birthday buddies," I say, to help our teacher 'cause she must have been mixed up to say that.

"But since February fifth is on a Saturday, we'll celebrate it tomorrow. And that means we get two birthday parties," Miss Hines explains.

This is back to being not good again.

"Whose parties?" asks Jason, my bestest friend who is a boy. "Nat's and who else?"

I am listening very hard to this answer. This is what *I* want to know. Who else is going to have a party on *my* birthday?

Miss Hines smiles big and turns that smile to the middle part of the second row.

Now my stomach feels more than bad twitchy. It feels like when I ate a whole stick of lipstick. Or a stick of butter. Or when I shared Percy's new cat food with him.

I think I know where our teacher is smiling at. Only I hope not.

Jason's question is still hanging in the air of our classroom, waiting for an answer.

Miss Hines gives the most horrible, awfullest answer she could come up with:

"Sasha."

Chapter 4

No Fair!

"But it's no *fair*, Mommy!"

We are in our car, Buddy, driving to the grocery store to get cupcake 'gredients.

"Why exactly isn't it fair, Nat?" Mommy asks.

"Two four isn't even Sasha's real birthday!" I tell her for the gazillionth time. My mom is very smart, except for sometimes like this. She should know that Sasha is just Sasha. Not Sasha 24.

"When *is* Sasha's birthday?" she asks.

"Her birthday is on Saturday, the *not*-February-four day. We are *not* birthday buddies."

"Guess she wanted a school party," Mommy says. "Friday *is* the closest school day to her birthday." She stops Buddy fast for a red light. She and I both sit up, then pop back in place. Sometimes it makes my stomach sick when Mommy drives Buddy.

Somebody honks a horn. I stare out the window. I have been hoping we'd get new snow for my birthday. The snow we have now is used snow. It's all dirty. Blackish snow mountains line up around the parking lots of Queen Burgers and Fish-O-Rama and the library.

"Natalie, tell me when your home birthday party is going to be."

Now I know my mom is having a bad day. She even wrote that birthday party date on all those invites. "Mommy, my real party is on Saturday. Don't you remember?"

She nods, then frowns back at me in the rearview mirror so I can see her frowny face.

The car behind us honks. The light's turned green. Mom jerks the car forward. "Nat, is *your* birthday on Saturday?"

Now I'm getting aggravated at *her*. "No! You know when my birthday is. Tomorrow! Friday."

"But you're having a party at our house on Saturday?" she asks, like this is a big surprise.

"Yes! You said to, so Daddy could come." I love my mom, but she is a big forgetter today.

She nods again. "Even though Saturday is Sasha's *real* birthday and not yours?"

Then I get it. She knew this all along. I hate it when she tries to get me to understand stuff I don't feel like understanding. "I get it," I admit.

But I still don't like it.

I stare out of Buddy's smudgy window and see three bigger boys racing fast on the sidewalk, where they're not supposed to ride bikes but they are. They have snowsuits on and stocking caps, but no gloves. One bike is red with a silver stripe. I like that bike.

"Mommy, can I have a big red bike with a silver stripe for my birthday?"

"No can do," Mommy answers.

"What *am* I getting for my birthday?" I ask.

Mommy sighs, but it sounds like air leaking out of a balloon. "I thought we agreed you wouldn't ask that question again, Nat."

We did agree this on account of my mom thought I asked that question a gazillion times a day. And she never answers it. So it was a waste of our brains to keep doing that.

"Yeah," I admit. "Only my birthday is tomorrow,

and I thought maybe that would be close enough. That's what."

"Nope," Mommy answers.

I don't know what I'm getting for my birthday. So far, I know I'm *not* getting a red bicycle with a silver stripe or a TV in my room or a pony.

I would very much love a pony.

Mom parks the car in the parking lot of the HyKlas Grocery Store. She parks very far away on account of a thing that happened one time.

One time I was in the car with my mom. And this is a story, but it is a true thing. Mom parked our car really up close to the grocery store, next to all the other close cars. Then we got our grocery stuff and got back into our car. Then she backed up our car. Only there was already a car there. So the two cars went "BANG! CRASH!"

And that happened one more time in this parking lot place.

So we park far away from those other cars now. And it is many, many steps to that grocery store.

Mommy helps me out of my booster seat. When I'm six tomorrow, I don't think I'll need this thing.

She holds my hand, and we look out for cars and hurry 'cause it's very cold. When I breathe, I make little frosty clouds. That's how cold it is.

When we are close to the HyKlas, I look up. And

then I see the most wonderful thing. "Mommy!" I shout. "There he is! There he is!"

"Nat, please," Mom says. "It's too cold."

She says something else, but I don't hear her. I don't see her. I don't see cars or people or anything. On account of what I do see.

My pony!

Chapter 5

Yellow Rocket

"Rocket!" I cry.

I love my horse that goes by the name of Rocket.

When Mom and I are on the sidewalk, I try to pull away from her and run to my horse. Only my mom is very strong. She keeps on holding my hand.

"Rocket! Rocket! Rocket!" I scream.

Rocket doesn't do anything, on account of he is made out of plastic. He can't move unless you feed him two quarters into his black box. Then he will

go fast like a rocket. That's where I got that name, *Rocket*.

"Nat," Mommy pleads, "it's freezing out here. You don't want to ride that thing now, do you?"

"Daddy would let me!" I shout. "Daddy *loves* horses!"

When my daddy takes me to the grocery store, we never get much groceries. He *always* lets me ride Rocket sometimes. Daddy puts quarters into Rocket's box and says, "I guess Rocket is a Quarter Horse." Then he laughs his head off. And I laugh too, so he doesn't feel bad.

I jerk my hand, and guess what! My hand comes out of my glove. So all Mom is holding is my glove. I race over to my horse and hug him around his hard neck. "I love you, Rocket," I tell him. He feels cold when I press my face to his. And kind of hard.

I pet Rocket. He looks like he used to be yellow and white before he got dirty like the snow.

When I was littler, I used to pretend yellow was my most favorite color. I loved purple best. But I felt sorry for yellow.

And here's why. When somebody asks, "What's your favorite color?" nobody answers, "Yellow." And that is 'cause yellow might as well be white, which is almost not really a color. Only yellow has a tiny bit of color in it. And not very much.

Not like purple. Laurie and I love purple and so do many, many girls. And mostly not boys. Boys don't like colors, except for some boys like black and maybe blue or green.

But nobody likes yellow. So I pretended I did.

I don't pretend that one anymore. Now I just love purple. One day, I'm going to paint my horse purple. That's what.

Mom has been saying hello to somebody. Only now she's done with that. She yells over at Rocket and me, "Please!"

I am getting a great birthday idea. "Mommy!" I shout. "Can I have Rocket for my very own for my birthday?" I should have thought of this great birthday idea before. "Ask Mr. HyKlas if we can buy Rocket!"

I hug Rocket again. "I will take you home, Rocket. Plus I will paint you purple. You can be my purple horse and live with me forever. In my room. With Percy, my cat."

"Now, Nat!" Mommy calls. "And the answer is no. You can't have Rocket for your birthday." She stamps her feet and blows into her gloves. "Nat, I'm freezing to pieces out here."

I am still hugging Rocket. But my fingers are freezing to pieces too. Especially my hand with no glove.

"Mommy, if I can't have Rocket for my birthday, can I ride Rocket now?" I ask.

"Not now, Nat. Maybe later," Mom says.

But I don't like "later." I hate "later."

"I *need* to ride Rocket *now*!" I tell her, on account of it feels like I do.

"Natalie?" Mommy's voice isn't Nice Mommy's voice. But I'm not Natalie Elizabeth yet. So I hug Rocket tighter.

"I need to ride Rocket now, Mommy." I don't say this very loud. But my words do that up-and-down thing that makes it sound almost like a song.

"Don't whine, Natalie," Mommy says.

I try not to whine. But when I say words again, they come out like that song thing. "I *need* to ride my horse!"

"Natalie Elizabeth," Mommy begins. This is how I know she's very aggravated at me. Which, in case you forgot, is what other mommies call mad. 'Sides, her eyes are little lines. "You do not *need* to ride that horse."

I *knew* she didn't understand, and this is proving it. "I *do*! I *need* to ride Rocket!" I say this part very loud 'cause I want her to understand this part very much. That's what.

I can tell by her line eyes that she does not understand this part.

She steps toward Rocket and me. "Natalie Elizabeth, I can see that you *want* to ride that horse. But you do not *need* to ride it. Understand?"

I shake my head in the no way because my stomach and my whole insides are feeling like *need*.

Mommy takes in air and lets it out. Like a leaky balloon. "Starving children *need* food. Someone wandering and lost in a desert *needs* water. Now do you understand?"

I stare at my mom because I think maybe she forgot all about Rocket. On account of she's worrying about the starving children in the desert.

"So," Mom goes on, like her mind isn't in a starving desert, "how about this? Since you *want* to ride the horse so much, I'll make you a deal."

This is not a good thing very much of the time. Mommy's deals are very hard. I wait for this deal.

"If you can be a good girl and go shopping without causing any trouble, then when we're done, you can ride the horse." Her eyes go back to Nice Mommy's round eyes that are very brown, like my eyes.

I look at Rocket. I look at Mommy. I look at Rocket. "Okay."

I let Mommy lead me by my hand toward the big glass doors that open all by themselves. There is still some sad in my heart about not riding Rocket *now*. I turn back to smile at my horse that I won't get for my birthday and that I didn't get to ride yet, even though I really needed to ride.

The grocery-store doors swish themselves open. Mommy jogs inside.

I turn back one more time to wave good-bye to Rocket.

And I see a horrible thing.

A very terrible, horrible thing.

Someone who's not me is climbing onto my horse.

She is wearing a purple coat.

That someone is that not-so-nice girl who is *not* my birthday buddy. That someone goes by the name of Sasha.

Sasha sits down on my horse, Rocket. Her mom puts quarters in the black box. Rocket goes up and down and back and front.

My feet stop moving.

"Nat?" Mommy says.

My eyes start crying. My head keeps looking back at my horse, Rocket.

Mommy pulls me into the HyKlas with her. The doors swoosh closed behind us.

The last thing I see is Sasha kicking the sides of my yellow horse, Rocket, and shouting, "Faster, you slow horse! Faster!"

Chapter 6

Purple Cakes

"Nat, this shopping trip is supposed to be fun,"
Mom says. She smiles at the people who stop and
look down at us before getting their grocery carts.

I have been standing here, crying about Rocket
and crying about Sasha. Only now I'm all out of cry.
I don't know how long it took, but those tears are
out of me.

"Remember our deal, Natalie?" Mommy asks.
She wipes my tears with her red gloves. "If you're
a good girl and help with the groceries, then you'll
get your turn on the horse. Right?"

I wish she hadn't said that about my horse. On
account of I think I was maybe wrong about those
tears being all out of me. There are some more left
in my head. Plus, they want out when my head
thinks about purple Sasha kicking yellow Rocket.

"Ready?" Mommy stands up because she was
kneeled down by me. She brushes grocery-store
dust off her pants and coat.

She grabs a big, shiny shopping cart, and I take
a little yellow cart. Only because that cart is so
yellow, it makes me think of my horse, Rocket. I

have to close my two eyes real fast so tears can't leak out my eye bulbs.

With my eyes closed, my brain still sees Sasha's purple coat sitting on my horse, Rocket. My yellow horse, Rocket. Today I will make yellow my favorite color. For Rocket, that's what. And purple will be my most unfavoritest color on account of Sasha's coat.

Only that doesn't go for tomorrow.

"Let's check out the bakery," Mommy says. "Maybe we can get some good ideas for cupcakes. Granny's coming over later."

I know this already. Granny and I are going to be baker ladies for my kindergarten cupcakes.

Mom walks along the glass bakery window, past cookies, to the cupcake section.

I push my favorite-color-yellow cart after her. Cookies go by me. I am almost to the cupcakes when I see something that makes my cart stop. There, in the middle of the top shelf, is the most beautiful cake I have ever seen. There are three cakes piled up into one cake, making stairsteps to the top. And that whole entire cake is purple, that's what. With pink and purplish flowers all around the outsides.

"Mommy! Mommy!" I cry. "Look at this!"

She walks back to where I am. My nose presses

on the cold glass so I can see this cake better. Right in the middle of that cake are big pink letters. I know those letters and even those words on account of I am a kindergarten girl. That cake says, "Happy Birthday!"

"Can I have that cake?" I ask my mom.

"Nat, Granny is making your birthday cake. You know that," Mom says.

I do know that. Granny and I are making cupcakes tonight. But my granny is making my real birthday cake all by herself for my Saturday party.

"But Granny doesn't make purple," I say. "Or flowers like these flowers."

Mom leans in for a better look. "I'm not even sure that cake's real. I think it's a model so people can order a cake like it."

This sounds like a very smart idea to me. "Let's order a cake like it!"

"Nat, we don't need a cake. Granny's making you a cake. That's much better than having a stranger make your cake, isn't it?"

I'm remembering the cake Granny made for my mom's birthday. It didn't have flowers. And it wasn't purple.

"Come on, Nat," Mommy says. "I need to get some milk."

"I want to stay and look at cakes."

She sighs. "Fine. Stay put. I'll be right up this aisle."

I hear Mom's boots *squeak, squeaking* and her cart *squeak, squeaking* away.

"Mother, is that *my* cake? They forgot to put my name on it!"

I know that voice, even before she starts shouting and crying. That voice belongs to Sasha. She runs up to the cake window and shoves me out of her way.

"See?" she screams at her mom. "It doesn't have my name on it! Or a six! Make them do it over."

Sasha's mom's shoes don't *squeak, squeak*. They *click-clack*. They are brown and pointy with skinny, long heels. "Now, sweetie," she says. Sasha's mom does not sound aggravated, even though Sasha is screaming like a not-so-nice girl. "That isn't your cake."

I can't help smiley-facing a little at this news. This purple cake is not mine, but it's also not Sasha's.

"I ordered a purple cake!" Sasha shouts. "Just like this one!"

"I know you did, honey," says her mom. "But we asked them to have it ready Saturday morning. Remember? I'm sure this one isn't your cake."

The baking lady comes over to the window.

She's wearing a white apron and a white hat 'cause that's what baker ladies wear in this HyKlas Grocery Store. "I remember you, young lady." This could be a good remember or a bad remember. "Your mother's right. I'll bake your cake myself for a Saturday eight a.m. pickup."

Sasha frowns at that purple cake. "So whose cake is this? *I'm* the one who gets a purple birthday cake. You can't let other people copycat my purple cake."

Sasha turns her frowny face to me. "Natalie, are you trying to buy this purple cake?"

"No," I answer. Only I wish very much I could say yes.

Sasha's eyes squeeze into little lines. "Do you promise?"

I squeeze *my* eyes into lines. "I don't have to promise."

"Mommy!" Sasha cries.

Sasha's mother runs up to her. "Now, sweetie. Nobody's going to have a birthday cake like yours." She tries to toss me a smiley face, but it's pretty much crooked. "Hello, Natalie. Are you and your mother shopping for your birthday cake?"

"My granny is making my birthday cake," I tell her.

"Is she, now?" says Sasha's mom.

"My granny is the best birthday-cake maker in the whole wide world," I tell her.

This is not so much a true thing. Last year my granny made me a brown birthday cake. She called it a volcano cake. On account of it fell inside itself when she took it out of the oven. Then the gooey insides oozed outside. But it tasted good.

"Well, isn't that nice," says Sasha's mother. She whispers something to Sasha.

"Good." Sasha smiles at me in a not-so-nice way.

I walk away to help my mom get milk. 'Cause guess what.

I am tired of looking at purple cakes.

Chapter 7

Store Samples

Leaving the cake window, I go past brownies. Past donuts. Past cupcakes. I feel frowny inside.

Only then I see something I had forgotten about in this grocery store. This something is the most wonderfullest thing about the HyKlas Grocery Store. Except for the horse outside.

Samples! That's what! They give away free food here and call it a "sample." Samples are where you can try out food before you eat it. I think this is a very good idea.

If I ever meet Mr. and Mrs. HyKlas, I will tell them so. Plus also, I will tell them that they should give sample horsey rides on Rocket. So I could see if I like those horsey rides.

A woman is standing behind a table full of samples in little plastic cups. Samples only come in tiny sizes. But you can have as many as you want. Mostly. If nobody is there to stop you.

"Would you like to taste our new fat-free bacon?" The sample lady smiles at somebody behind me.

I turn around to see my mom there.

"Go ahead, Nat," she says. "I was thinking of switching to this brand. See how you like it."

Mom takes a sample and eats it first. "That's good." She asks the lady some questions about fat.

I take the cup with the biggest sample in it. I hold the cup high and drop the sample into my mouth.

I chew on this sample. It isn't juicy like our old bacon. It tastes kind of like Laurie's pencil. Or rubber bands.

I don't want this rubber pencil taste to go down to my stomach. It might stay there, tasting rubbery all night.

I want this yucky taste *out*.

I spit the rubbery bacon sample back into the plastic cup.

Only I miss. Because that cup is so tiny. That's what. 'Sides, I already squished that cup on accident.

"Natalie," Mom says in a not-happy voice.

"I'm sorry." I pick up the rubber pencil bacon

from the floor. My mom makes aggravated eyebrows at me.

I don't want her to think I'm not keeping our deal about being good and getting to ride on yellow Rocket.

I can still taste that rubbery. But I think about Rocket. I love that horse, Rocket.

I take a giant breath, close my eyes, throw back my head, and dangle that rubbery, chewed-up bacon over my open mouth.

"No!" shout my mom and the sample lady at the same time.

I open my eyes. I close my mouth.

"You can throw it in here," the lady says. She holds out a plastic wastebasket.

I do that. "That wastebasket is a very good idea," I tell the sample lady. And I'm thinking I'm not the only sample taster to spit this stuff out.

Mom heads for the next grocery street. I follow her, but I'm hunting for more samples.

The best samples are always back in the bakery part of the grocery store. But they keep those samples way up high. This is another thing I would like to talk to Mr. and Mrs. HyKlas about.

On the top of the cookie counter I can see a big plate. I know there are sample cookies and cakes on there. But they are too much high up to reach. Even by jumping.

And even if you stand inside of your yellow cart on your tippytoes, you cannot reach those yummy samples. I know this for true 'cause I tried that one.

I walk over to the bread. Sometimes Mr. and Mrs. HyKlas get mixed up and put good samples over there.

And sure enough, there is one. It's a plate with a plastic bubble top. Plus I can reach that plate.

I lift off the bubble top, and there are sample brownies in there! Plus also, there is not even a sample lady guarding these brownies.

My tummy is grumbling. It wants very much to try out these brownies, so I try out one.

Then I try out another one.

And those two samples are so yummy that I try out two more at the same time.

"Hey! Leave some for the rest of us!" This mean thing is said by Sasha. She has a yellow cart that is heading for my samples.

I want to say something kind of mean to Sasha. Only I can't because my mouth is full up with brownie samples. Words won't fit in there.

Sasha's mother *click-clacks* up to the brownie samples. "Would you like to try a brownie, Sasha?" she asks.

"Yes, please," Sasha says. She takes a big sample her mom hands her right into her mouth. "I like it. Can we buy some? Can we? We need more snacks for my birthday party."

I wait for Sasha's mom to tell her about whining and not needing brownies if you're not in the desert starving.

But Sasha's mom just takes a sample herself and says, "Of course, honey. Good idea."

I look around for my mom, so she can tell them about the desert. But Mommy is talking to a lady from church who talks a lot.

I guess it's up to me. I turn back around to tell Sasha about the desert kids. Only I'm too late.

Sasha takes the last sample off that sample plate and stuffs it into her big mouth. That's what.

Chapter 8

Worm Juice

We end up at the checking-out counter the exactly same time Sasha and her mom get there. My mom lets Sasha's mom go first. This is a mistake. On account of we have to watch them unload both of their shopping carts.

Sasha's cart: A gazillion brownies in a big white box. A gazillion cookies in plastic boxes. Bags of balloons. Packages of bouncy balls. Packs of Old Maid cards. Toys. Games.

Sasha's mom's cart: A gazillion cupcakes with purple icing. Another gazillion cupcakes with rainbow icing. Another gazillion cupcakes with white icing and sprinklies. Other white boxes I can't see through.

I stop watching 'cause it makes my stomach twitchy to see all that stuff.

My mom reaches for the white stick that keeps different people's foods from getting mixed up. She sets the stick on the black moving checking-out counter to keep our stuff away from Sasha's stuff.

Sasha and her cart are in front of me. Mommy and her cart are behind me. I don't have my yellow cart. 'Sides, it was empty. Plus I forgot it somewhere in the HyKlas.

My mom starts unloading her cart. Here's what's in Mommy's cart: three boxes with pictures of cake on them, juice boxes, napkins, a bag of sugar, a bag of powdery sugar, and butter.

There are more grocery things in Mommy's cart. But they are very boring.

Between the checking-out place and the outside doors, there is a sample table. I didn't see it when we came in 'cause of tears in my eyes.

I have to walk around Sasha and her mom and their food to get to the sample table.

"Don't go outside, Nat," Mommy calls.

"I won't," I call back. This is a true thing. I am rule-keeping Natalie 24. On account of I made that deal about riding my horse, Rocket.

On this sample table, there are tiny plastic cups of green drink. It could be lemonade.

I pick up one of those could-be lemonades. This makes me remember that I am very thirsty. I slurp in a big mouthful of green. Only I don't swallow. On account of this is NOT lemonade.

It stinks and tastes exactly like green worm juice.

The sample lady comes running over to me. Her face looks like *she's* the one who drank this stuff. "Oh, honey. This is for people playing sports. Runners drink it so they won't get dehydrated."

I don't know what that means. But nobody should have to drink this stuff.

The worm juice is stuck in my mouth. It won't go down the rest of me. My stomach is shouting, "Don't you send that junk down here!"

And my mouth is shouting back, "Well, I'm not keeping that stuff in here!"

Right then, somebody's little cart smack-a-roos into the back of me. *Pow!*

Green stuff sprays out of my mouth like a super-shooter.

"Gross!" Sasha is standing behind me.

I wheel around on her. "You did that on purpose!"

"Did not." She pulls purple gloves out of her purple coat pockets and puts them on.

I make my eyes into lines like Mommy when she's aggravated. "*You* ran into me!" I shout.

Green worm juice is all over the floor. People are walking around that mess.

"Clean up on Aisle One!" comes the big fat 'nouncement for the whole entire HyKlas to hear.

Sasha's mom comes running over and takes Sasha's hand. "Let's go to the car, sweetheart," she says.

Two grocery men follow Sasha and her mother out the door. Each of the grocery men has a special cart with Sasha's groceries.

A boy in a white apron wipes the worm juice off the floor.

I bend myself down and whisper to him, "I'm really sorry I made a mess. I was trying out the sample. And Sasha ran into me. And that green stuff wouldn't stay in my mouth. On account of it tastes like worm juice."

He winks at me. "Yeah. They should put a warning on the label, if you ask me." Then he walks off with his broom and rag. I think he is a very smart boy.

Mommy comes running over with our groceries. "Natalie, is everything all right?"

"Yep. Can I ride Rocket now? Please?" I add. 'Cause that's the nice way to ask things.

She smiles. "I guess you better take your last ride as a five-year-old. Huh, Nat?"

Together, we push the silver cart with our grocery bags in it. Instead of pushing to the car, we go straight to Rocket.

"Here I come, Rocket!" I shout. I climb up on Rocket's back and hug his neck.

It's very hard waiting for Mommy to find her quarters for my Quarter Horse. Finally, she drops two quarters into the black box.

I grab the reins. "Giddyup, Rocket!"

Rocket doesn't giddyup.

"He needs more monies, Mommy," I tell her.

"I put in two quarters." She goes through the whole purse hunt again. She finds two more quarters and puts them in. They clunk, clunk into the money hole on the black box.

I am so excited that my heart is thumpy.

Only Rocket still doesn't go.

"Giddyup, Rocket! Please!" I bounce up and down on his back. I lean way forward. "Go!"

He doesn't.

Mommy pushes a silver button on the box.

Nothing happens. "I guess it's broken," she says.

"No!" I saw Rocket working before. A very bad picture comes into my brain. Purple on yellow. Sasha on Rocket.

Mommy bangs on the black box. "It won't even give me my money back. Come on. Let's go home. I'm freezing."

I climb off of my horse, Rocket. "I'm sorry, Rocket," I whisper. My neck is chokey.

Mommy pushes our cart through the parking lot. "Maybe it's too cold for the horse ride to work."

I look back over my shoulder at Rocket. I know it's not the cold's fault that my horse, Rocket, won't work. And I know whose fault it is.

Sasha's. That's what.

Chapter 9

Humming, Cupcake-Making, Present-Opening Girls

Mommy and I leave the cupcake groceries out on the counter. We put the boring groceries away. My heart is so thumpy about making cupcakes that it's really hard to wait for Granny.

Daddy, Mommy, and I eat fried chicken while we're waiting. We're all done when somebody knocks at the door.

"Granny's here!" I run to the door and open it. And I'm right.

Granny is standing there with her arms full up with bags. "Cupcakes for kindergarten coming right up!" She marches in, shouting, "Cupcakes for kindergarten! Cupcakes for kindergarten!"

I love my granny.

Mom takes Granny's coat. Daddy gets Granny's bags. Then we go to the kitchen. On account of Granny says we need to get down to business. That's what.

"Are you sure you don't want me to help?" Mom asks.

"You know what they say about too many cooks,

Kelly," Granny answers.

"Ah. Got it." Mom leaves, but she's smiley-faced.

But I don't get it. "What do they say about too many cooks?"

"Too many cooks spoil the cupcakes," Granny whispers.

When Granny and I are alone in the kitchen, she starts humming. I know that humming song. We sing that song in our church. So I hum too.

"We are humming cupcake girls," I tell Granny between hums.

"Humming cupcake girls, who can't carry a tune in a bucket." Granny laughs. Then we hum another God song. It goes by the name of "Jesus Loves Me."

I love that song. And even without the words, our humming sounds like "Jesus Loves Me."

Granny dumps cake powder from the box into a giant big bowl. She smashes two eggs and plops them into the powdery. Then she pours some oil into a cup and lets me dump that one in.

We take turns stirring. And stirring harder. We don't even use a stirring machine like Mom uses. On account of we are old-fashioned humming cupcake girls.

Granny looks both ways like she's crossing a street. Only I think she's making sure we're all by ourselves. "Ready for my secret ingredient?" she whispers.

I nod. My heart gets a little thumpy. I love secret 'gredients.

"Chocolate chips," she whispers.

"Wow!" I whisper back.

Granny points to one of the bags she made Daddy carry to the kitchen. "Bring me the chips, Nat. Your daddy used to love my cupcakes with chocolate chips when he was a boy."

I look in one bag, but I don't see the chips. I'm thinking about how many birthdays my dad had when he was a boy. Plus also, how many my granny had. "How old are you, Granny?" I ask.

"A lady never tells her age," Granny answers.

"But that old whale, Moby Dick, was a tadpole when I was born."

Sometimes my granny doesn't make sense.

I peek into the next bag. Only there aren't any chocolate chips in there. Plus there are two presents in that bag.

"Granny! Are these for me?"

Granny comes over to the presents. "Hmm . . . well, let's see. Who's going to have a birthday tomorrow?"

"Me!"

"Guess these are yours, then."

"Can I open them now?" I make my eyes big at Granny. Sometimes that works with her. My mom never ever lets me open a present early. But Granny is a maybe. "Please? Please, Granny?"

I can tell by my granny's eyes that she wants me to open these presents. "Your birthday isn't until tomorrow," she says.

"But you won't be here in the morning when I open my presents," I remind her. "And you *are* here now."

"Good point," Granny admits. She reaches into the bag and pulls out a box.

It might could hold a mouse. Or a hat. Or shoes. Or a hamburger. But not a TV. Or a horse. Or a bike.

"Let's open one." Granny whispers this like we are secret present-opening girls.

I pull off the purple bow. I rip off the cat paper. I tear open the box. "Wow!" Inside is a silvery thing, like metal circles sitting on top of each other. It could be a big, fat bracelet.

"It's so filled with gorgeousness!" I hug my granny. "Thank you, Granny."

I stare at this silver thing. Then I pull it out of the box. Only it gets bigger when I pull it, like a big, silvery circles snake.

"It's a Slinky, Nat," Granny explains.

I like that word, *slinky*.

Granny takes my silvery Slinky out of the box and walks to the basement steps with it. I follow her.

"Watch this," Granny says. She turns on the light. She sets the Slinky thing on the top step. And she pushes it.

"Granny!" I don't want my new present pushed into the basement.

"Watch," Granny says.

I watch. The Slinky plops one silvery circle onto the next step. It looks like a fat worm doing that. Then the other circles slinky down to that step too. Only the top circle plops to the next step. And the whole Slinky slinks over itself and down to the next step. My Slinky slinks down those stairs all by itself.

"Wowee! Wow!" I trot down the steps after my present. It's standing still, like in the box. I pick it up and climb the stairs back to the kitchen. "I love this Slinky thing, Granny!"

"Better put it back for now, Nat," Granny says. "This weekend we'll go to the mall and introduce Mr. Slinky to Miss Escalator."

Granny and I get back to work on cupcakes. It takes both of us to stir in chocolate chips. We pour the chocolaty stuff into the wavy paper cups that look like upside-down skirts. Then we wait for the oven to cook.

Pretty soon the whole kitchen, plus also, the

whole house, smells like cupcakes. This is one great smell. A birthday smell.

Granny and I make frosting with many secret 'gredients. I lick all the bowls and spoons. Except Granny gets the wood spoon.

A gazillion minutes happen. Then Granny takes the cupcakes out of the oven. "Not bad," she says.

"They look yummy!" I say. "And chocolaty."

"And hot," Granny says.

We have to wait for them to not be hot before we put frosting on. Another gazillion minutes happen.

Finally, Granny 'nounces, "They're all set." She gives me a not-sharp knife and a bowl of frosting. "Go to it, Nat."

I go to it. I dip in the knife and come out with a glob of chocolate frosting. Then I plop it onto the first cupcake. But when I try to spread the frosting, cake globs onto the knife. "Granny, I'm ruining it!" I shout, on account of there's a big, fat hole in my cupcake.

"Try another one," Granny says.

I try another one. The same thing happens. Cupcake globs hang on my frosting knife. "I'm a terrible cupcake frostinger, Granny."

"Nonsense," Granny says. "You're doing just fine."

I try three more cupcakes. Only I tear their

crumbly heads off. "I hate this stupidhead frosting."

"Keep at it," Granny says. "Practice makes perfect."

I keep trying. And I keep messing up. "Granny, practice isn't making them perfect."

Granny chuckle-laughs.

But I don't. On account of this is not funny.

Tomorrow is my school birthday party. And I am in serious cupcake trouble. That's what.

Chapter 10

Happy Birthday to ME, That's What!

I wake up before the sun and moon switch places. I can tell this about the sun and moon on account of I have a window in the wall of my bedroom.

"Percy!" I whisper-shout. "It's my happy birthday!"

Percy doesn't answer.

Percy never answers very often.

He stays curled up where my feet usually go in my bed. The moon pokes light through my window right onto Percy. He looks like a ball of white fluffy down there.

"Percy?" I say more loud.

He doesn't answer again.

There are some dark shapes left in my bedroom from the night. They look like bad people. And monsters. Only not.

A night creaky noise happens by my closet.

Part of me feels like it would be a very good idea to pull up my covers over my head so I don't see the dark.

Or hear the dark.

But the new, six-year-old Natalie 24 in me says to those dark shapes, "Happy birthday to *me*!" And jumps out of bed.

"Come on, Percy 24." I lift up my cat and carry him all the way to Mom and Dad's room. Percy and I open the door. We tippytoe in.

There are many snores in Mom and Dad's bed. Percy and I climb up. We crawl on our hands and knees between Mom and Dad. Then we say, "Happy birthday to me!"

"Wh-what?" Daddy sits up fast. Percy jumps off the bed.

Mom's eyes pop open. "Nat?"

I wait for them to be waked up more. Then they can say, "Happy birthday!"

"What time is it?" Daddy asks.

"Time for my birthday," I answer.

Daddy plops his head back on his pillow.

Mommy sits up in bed. "Happy birthday, Nat."

She yawns and turns their alarm clock to her. "Let's let Daddy sleep a little longer. Come on. We'll make a birthday breakfast."

"With real bacon?" I'm pretty sure Mommy didn't buy the rubber kind.

"You bet, Nat."

"Happy birthday," Daddy says. I think. 'Cause he says it into his pillow.

We have a whole lot of morning before it's time to go to school. Mom and I make pancakes and bacon. We pack me a special lunch with two cupcakes. One for me and one for my bestest friend, Laurie. Only I also stick in two more. One for Farah and one for Anna.

We pack up our classroom party cupcakes. They are filled with fanciness. Granny covered up all of my frosting mess-ups with pink and purple sprinklies.

Mom packs enough cupcakes so everybody in our class can have two. Even Sasha and even Peter. I can carry the plastic boxes to school myself, just like other birthday kids in our class did before. On account of I am six. That's what.

Daddy gets up. "Hey! Happy birthday, birthday girl. How come nobody woke me up?"

"We did!" I give him a birthday hug.

Mom goes to her secret hiding place. And she

comes out with presents. For me!

I open the biggest present first. It's a giant stuffed dinosaur. I hug it. "Steg-O is going to love you!" Steg-O is my little dinosaur.

I hug Mommy and Daddy really hard. "Thank you! It's what I always wanted. And I didn't even know that."

Plus also, I get a toy that has a screen and buttons to push. And noise. It's really a learning thing. But I like it anyway.

I get two games. I can't hardly wait to play these games with Laurie. Plus also, clothes. These are not usually good presents. Only one of those clothes is a purple jogging suit, and I love it. "Can I wear these purple clothes to school?"

"Good idea," Mom answers.

I'm opening the other present from Granny when the phone rings. And guess who is on that phone? Granny! I know that Different Granny and Gramps will call me too. Only later 'cause they live way far away in California. And time is all mixed up in that place. It's probably not even my birthday yet there.

"How's my birthday girl?" Granny asks.

"I love being six, Granny! Plus I have presents. And I've been up for a very long time. I'm opening your other present that's for me."

"Good timing then, huh?" I think she yawns into the phone.

I open the present and scream, "I love it, Granny! Thank you!" It's a purple sweatshirt with three big cats on the front. The cats have on cowboy hats and cowboy boots. "They're cowboy cats!"

"Have you looked on the back yet?" Granny asks.

I turn the shirt to its back. And the backs of those three big cats are on the back of my sweatshirt. "Wow!"

"Glad you like it, Nat." I think I hear her yawn again. "Best wear that one at home, though. Never know how a teacher will take to a shirt with cats' backsides on the back, if you know what I mean."

"I have our cupcakes ready to go," I tell her. "They look fancy."

"Well, you deserve fancy. Have a great time at kindergarten."

"Yep." I know I will. It's Month Number Two and Day Number Four. And I, Natalie 24, get my own kindergarten birthday party.

On account of I am a lucky birthday girl. That's what.

Chapter 11

The Cupcake Crash

"Nat, are you sure you don't want me to help you carry in your treats?" Mommy asks.

"No thanks. I can do it myself." I saw other birthday kids carry in their own parties.

We are in Buddy in the school car parking lot. I'm trying to climb out of the backseat. Only my backpack is full of juice boxes and napkins. And I have two big plastic boxes of cupcakes to carry.

Jason, my bestest friend who is a boy, and not my boyfriend, runs by the car. Then he runs back. He is a runner boy. "Happy birthday, Nat!" he shouts.

"Thanks, Jason."

"Maybe Jason can help you carry things in," Mom says.

Jason must hear her 'cause he sticks out his arms for me to put something in. Only his feet are still moving. He is not a standing-still boy. Plus he is sometimes a dropping-things boy. On account of he runs everywhere.

I don't want to give Jason my fancy cupcakes. "Would you carry my backpack?" I ask Jason.

"It's purple!" he shouts. "Purple is a girl color."
He holds his nose. "I can't touch purple."

"Oh, all right." I hand Jason both boxes of
cupcakes. Then I take one back. "Be careful, Jason.
Promise?"

"Don't worry!" Jason shouts. He is also a shouter
boy. "I won't let anybody steal these cupcakes! I am
the cupcake police!" He takes off running.

"Wait!" I holler.

"Natalie?" Mom rolls down Buddy's window.
"Everything okay?"

"Yeah." Only I'm not so sure about that. I'm
watching Jason run a whole circle around Buddy.
"Careful, Jason," I say when he comes by me again.

"Well, have a happy birthday party. Okay?"
Mom starts up Buddy.

I wave good-bye to Mom and Buddy. Then I
try to catch up with Jason. Only I don't want to run
and shake up my cupcakes.

Jason is way ahead of me. He's running on the
sidewalk toward school. He dodges a bigger boy.
He races around a littler girl.

"I am a cupcake cop!" Jason shouts.

"Don't run, Jason!" I shout at him. But he is
really far ahead of me now. "Jason!" I yell louder.

Jason turns back around to face me. Only his feet
can't stop running. He's running backwards. "Your

cupcakes are safe with me, Nat!"

But I see what's behind Jason. And Jason doesn't see what's behind Jason. There is a Jason-sized boy walking very slow up the sidewalk. His back is to Jason. Their backs are getting closer and closer on account of Jason is running backwards.

"Jason, look out!" I cry.

Crash!

Jason smacks into the other boy's back.

The boy falls down. Jason's feet fly up off the sidewalk. He tips backwards. Then he crashes on top of the other boy.

I watch the white plastic box of cupcakes fly out of Jason's hands. It sails up, up, up, and then does a Slinky-flip down into a pile of dirty, used snow.

"My cupcakes!" I scream.

I run for those cupcakes. Only then I remember I have cupcakes too. So I hug my box of cupcakes and walk really fast—only careful—to that snow pile.

Jason is okay. He gets there before I do. He reaches for the cupcake box.

"Don't touch it!" I yell. I pick up the box and brush off the snow.

"Cool!" Jason shouts. "The top didn't even come off. We still got cupcakes in there."

Only the cupcakes are down-side up. "They're all smushed." My neck is chokey, looking at those smushy things. Some are stuck to the box. "They're ruined!"

"They look okay to me. *I'll* eat 'em," Jason says. He reaches for the box.

I jerk it away from him. The cupcakes *thud* against the box. Some are sticking to the lid. I stick the box of ruined cupcakes under the box of still-good cupcakes. I make a frowny face at Jason, then stomp away.

Jason whizzes past me. He doesn't say sorry. He

runs into school without holding the door open for me to get in.

I have to stand at the door until a kid comes out. Then I scoot into school with my boxes of cupcakes. A smushed box. And a not-smushed box.

"Happy birthday, Nat!" Laurie yells up the hall. When she reaches me, she asks, "What's the matter?"

"Jason." I have to swallow the chokey in my neck. "He dropped my cupcakes. They're all smushed."

Laurie peeks in at the top cupcakes. "They look great, Nat."

"Not those. The underneath ones."

Laurie peeks in at those underneath cupcakes. "They're pretty smushed, all right. But you've got so many cupcakes. You can pass out the good ones first. Most kids will just take one."

"Yeah?" I didn't know this. I always take two.

"Yeah!" Laurie takes both boxes from me. I let her. On account of she is not a running girl or a dropping-things girl.

Laurie and I walk into our classroom. Kids run up to see what we brought.

"Don't the cupcakes look great!" Laurie says, keeping the not-smushed box on top of the smushed one.

I look around the room to see if Sasha's here yet with *her* cupcakes. I spot her by Ham the Hamster's cage. Everybody else is checking out my cupcakes, except for Sasha. I don't see any other cupcakes in this room. What if Sasha doesn't have birthday cupcakes?

I feel a tiny bit of sad for Sasha. Maybe her mother made her save up all that grocery-store food for her real birthday. Maybe Sasha doesn't have party cupcakes for kindergarten. If I didn't have party cupcakes, even smushed ones, I would feel bad. That's what.

I ask Jesus about this. On account of he's in this kindergarten place too. Not just in church. Or at the HyKlas. Then I decide I will let Sasha pass out some of my cupcakes.

Maybe the smushed ones.

I take another look at Sasha. She's still all alone with Ham. Maybe she can help pass the not-smushed cupcakes too.

Anna and Farah crowd in closer. They stare in at the top cupcakes, which have many sprinklies on there to hide my frosting goof-ups.

"The cakes are beautiful," Farah says. I like how Farah talks. Her words sound more beautifuller than most kids'. Like she picks out each word from a special place before she lets the word out of her mouth.

"Thanks, Farah," I tell her. "Granny and I used lots of sprinklies."

"You *made* these?" Anna asks. "Did you get to lick the bowl?"

"Yep."

Laurie sets the cupcakes down on the edge of the teacher's desk. Miss Hines waves to us. But she's busy getting kids out of their coats.

Sasha finally comes over to look. She stares at the box of not-smushed cupcakes. But her frowny face looks like she's staring at the smushed cupcakes.

Laurie says, "I think these cupcakes are the most gorgeous cupcakes I've ever seen."

Sasha makes a noise that could be an evil laugh. "That's because you haven't seen *my* cupcakes yet."

Chapter 12

Birthday Buddies . . . Not!

"What are you bringing for *your* class party, Sasha?"
Bethany asks.

"You'll have to wait and see," Sasha answers.

"How come you didn't bring in your own
cupcakes, like Nat did?" Laurie asks.

"There was too much for me to carry," Sasha
answers. "My mother has to drive in with all of our
classroom party stuff later. She's going to help Miss
Hines put on the party."

This is a very not-fair thing. *My* mother doesn't
get to be a party-putting-on-er.

"Class?" Miss Hines walks to the front of the
room. She gets very big in her eyes when she sees
my cupcake box.

"Mmm . . . looks good," Miss Hines says. She
puts the boxes behind her desk, where we can't see
them. "Now, I'd like you to take your seats, please."

"Take 'em where?" Jason shouts. He has said
this joke a gazillion times.

So I don't bother laughing. Plus also, I'm still
aggravated at Jason for ruining my cupcakes.

"I think we should start our day by singing

'Happy Birthday' to our birthday buddies, don't you?" Miss Hines says.

I want to tell her that I don't have a birthday buddy. I want to tell her that it's no fair that Sasha's mother is bringing more food than Sasha can carry.

Miss Hines stands in front of her giant desk. "Sasha and Natalie, will you girls please stand up so we can sing to you?"

This is one of those questions we're not supposed to answer. Sasha is already standing up. I stand up.

Miss Hines starts off the singing.

But everybody else takes over.

From the other side of the room, I hear Jason's shouting voice. He is singing his own words to this

song: "Happy Smurf-Day! Tee-hee! You're as blue as can be. You need glasses to see. Happy Smurf-Day! Tee-hee!"

It makes me laugh to hear Jason's made-up words. Until I remember I'm aggravated at that shouting boy.

The singing is done, so I sit down. Several kids turn around and say, "Happy birthday!" at me. I am kinda feeling like a birthday girl again.

Sasha is still standing up. "Miss Hines?"

"Yes, Sasha," says our teacher.

"I have an announcement," Sasha says.

She can't make a 'nouncement. *Teachers* make 'nouncements. Sasha is *not* our teacher.

I wait for Miss Hines to tell Sasha this.

Only Miss Hines doesn't. She says, "Well . . ."

And Sasha goes ahead and says her 'nouncement anyway. "I'd just like to say that we're going to have the best birthday party ever in this class when my mother gets here."

"That's fine, Sasha," Miss Hines says. "You can take your seat—"

"*And*," Sasha goes on instead of taking her seat, "tomorrow I'm having a *real* birthday party."

I am having a *real* birthday party tomorrow too. Before right now, I didn't even think about Sasha's party and my party being on the same day. Now I am thinking about this. I wonder if Sasha will come to my party first. Or last. Or if maybe the parties are at the same time.

Sasha is still talking. "I'll be inviting some of you. But not all of you. I can only invite fifteen kids to my party. My mother is sorry about that. She says it's the party planner's rule and not hers."

Sasha makes a smiley face all around the room. "So don't feel so bad if you don't get an invitation. There would be too many of us for the horse rides if everybody came."

A couple of kids gasp.

"Horse rides?" Bethany repeats.

"And the jumping boxes," Sasha adds.

"Cool!" Peter yells.

Miss Hines's eyes turn to lines. "Sasha, this is not the place to—"

"I'm almost done," Sasha says. She holds up a bunch of letters that look like they have Christmas cards inside. "Not everybody in this room will get one of these. But at least you'll have a super party today when my mother gets here." She takes one of the invitations and hands it to Peter.

A gazillion hands go up to get one of those things.

"Stop!" Miss Hines walks back to Sasha's desk. "Take your seat, Sasha."

Finally, Sasha does.

"I don't want you passing out invitations in this classroom. Do you understand me?" Miss Hines has her mean-teacher voice on. She turns to the whole class. "Quiet. We have work to do."

She has to say this on account of kids are whispering. It sounds like bumbly bees in here.

Only I am not bumbly. I am not whispering. I am thinking in my head.

My brain is seeing that big purple cake in the grocery store. Only now it has Sasha's name on it. She's getting a big, purple grocery-store birthday cake for her party.

And I'm not.

Sasha is having jumping boxes at her party.

And I'm not.

Sasha is having horse rides at her party.

And I'm not.

Real horse rides. With horses that aren't plastic and yellow and don't need quarters to make them move.

I look around our classroom. Sasha is having the kind of birthday party every kid in kindergarten will want to go to.

And I'm not.

Chapter 13

Two Parties Too Many

"Nat! Hurry up! I saved you a swing." My bestest friend, Laurie, yells this to me at recess. She is a great swing saver.

I shuffle my feet to the swing set. This is the first time we've had recess outdoors for a long time. It took us half our recess time to get on our outside clothes.

I take the middle swing Laurie saved.

Anna is swinging on the other side of me. She already had her birthday party in our class. She passed out napkins that came from China on account of her granny still lives in that place.

Somebody screams. I look fast and see a girl from our class who goes by the name of Erika. She is jumping up and down and waving something in her hand.

"One more invitation," Anna says. Her boots squeak when she drags them to stop her swinging. "Sasha passed out a bunch already. There can't be too many left."

Sasha is standing in the middle of the playground. A gazillion kids are crowding around her.

I hear Bethany's voice. "What about me, Sasha? Is there one for me?"

Yesterday Bethany said she was coming to *my* party.

"Hmmm," Sasha says. "Bethany . . . Bethany . . . Let me see." She goes through the invitation envelopes she's still got left. "I don't know . . ."

Bethany is kind of dancing next to Sasha. She tries to peek at the cards. But Sasha jerks them away. "Is it there?" Bethany whines. "Am I invited?"

"Well, look at this," Sasha says. She holds a card to her chest. Then she hands it to Bethany.

"YEA!" Bethany grabs the card and rips it open. "I got one!"

"Big deal," Anna mutters. "Who cares?" She drags one boot on the ground. Her swing spins in a slow circle.

I'm glad that Anna doesn't care about getting invited to Sasha's party. She's coming to *my* party.

Laurie must be thinking what I'm thinking 'cause she says to Anna, "We're going to play all kinds of games at Nat's party."

Anna makes a tiny smiley face at us. "That will be—"

"Anna!" Sasha tromps right in front us. "I've been looking for you."

"For me?" Anna says.

Sasha holds up an envelope. She reads the front of it. "Is your name Anna?"

"Yes! I'm Anna."

Sasha hands over an invitation. Anna takes it like it's a big, fancy Christmas present. "Thanks, Sasha!" Anna says. "I can't believe you invited *me*!"

Sasha makes a smiley face. But she turns that face to me. And it doesn't look smiley for real. "I just wish I had enough invitations so everyone could get one."

I stare at the invitations Sasha is still holding. I think they're all gone, except for one. Sasha is hiding that one, last envelope against her purple coat.

Laurie makes her eyes into lines and turns her frowny face to Sasha. "Sasha, what time is your party?"

"The party starts at nine in the morning," Sasha answers.

This is exactly when *my* party starts. My mom wrote on all the invites *Party time: 9–11, Saturday morning*. That way we don't have to make lunch. Only maybe we can change my party time. On account of Sasha's party is then.

Before I can say this idea, Laurie comes up with it. "Nat, do you think your mom would switch your party to after lunch instead? Kids could go to both parties."

Sasha shakes her head. "That won't work."

"Why not?" Laurie asks.

"Because *my* party is all day. We do party stuff at my house in the morning," Sasha explains.

"Like horse rides? And jumping-on-the-trampoline things?" Anna asks. She sounds way too excited about these things for a girl who will be at my party then.

"And other things too," Sasha says. "Lots of secret surprises."

My neck is getting chokey. This is why I leave the talking to my bestest friend.

"And all that stuff is in the morning, right?" Laurie asks. She turns to Anna. "So maybe you can go to Sasha's in the morning and come over to Nat's in the afternoon."

"I'd like that," Anna says.

"But you'll miss the Pizza Game Parlor," Sasha says.

"The Pizza Game Parlor?" Anna shouts. "Wow! I've always wanted to go there!"

Now I am chokey all over. That pizza place has games like Skee-Ball and a fish tank and machines you sit in and drive. Plus also, pizza.

"Well," Laurie tries, "you can't stay there all afternoon, can you?"

I think this is a good point. I just hope it's okay with Mom and Dad and Granny if we have my party later.

"Of course we can't stay there all afternoon," Sasha says. "That's why my dad reserved the whole bowling alley for later."

Even Laurie gets big in her eyes at that one. I know she's trying not to, on account of I know my friend that much. And 'cause I know Laurie so much, I know that Laurie LOVES to go bowling. And she never gets to go almost, 'cause there are too many people in Laurie's family and not enough bowling money.

Laurie doesn't talk after this bowling news. She just makes a frowny face at Anna. Then a frownier face at Sasha. Then an I'm-sorry face at me.

"Oh." Sasha pulls out her very last invite card. "Almost forgot." She hands that last invite to my bestest friend, Laurie. "This is for you."

Chapter 14

Downhill from There

"Cheer up, Nat," Laurie says when we're eating in the cafeteria.

All around us, everybody is talking about Sasha's party.

"You know I'd never go anywhere but to *your* party," Laurie promises.

I thought this. That's how bestest friends are. Only it's very good to hear this in person. "Really, Laurie?"

"Of course!" Laurie answers.

"But what about bowling?" Once, Laurie said she'd rather bowl than color. And she *loves* to color.

Laurie takes a big bite of her sprinkly cupcake. "It wouldn't be any fun without you." That's what I think she says. But it's hard to tell with her cupcake mouth.

Laurie finishes her cupcake. "Kids are going to figure out the same thing, Nat. They know your party will be more fun 'cause *you're* more fun than Sasha."

"I am?"

"Sure." Laurie snaps her lunch box shut. "So, let's have a great classroom party. I can't wait to eat another one of your cupcakes! Remember what your granny always says."

I try to remember. But Granny says a lot of stuff. "What?"

"Keep your chin up. That way you'll see God—or heaven, I can't remember exactly—and everything else will start looking up too."

Laurie's right. Granny does say that. Only she also has a saying about things going from bad to worse. And one that goes, "If you think things can't get worse, use your imagination." Plus also, other sayings about things going downhill. Like, "Things went downhill from there."

Miss Hines has us finish our work early. Then she says, "Class, will you please clear your desks?"

Our teacher gives me her best smiley face and says, "While we're waiting for Sasha's mother to join us, Natalie, I'd like you to pass out your treats."

My heart gets very thumpy. "I have napkins in my pack. And juice boxes in my cubby."

"Sounds great!" Miss Hines says. "Why don't you pick a partner to help you pass out your goodies, Natalie."

This is a great idea. I smile at my bestest friend. "Laurie!" Of course.

Laurie passes out juice, and I pass out napkins. Then we both go get the not-smushed cupcake box from our teacher. We each take one side of the box.

I am starting to think that Laurie picked the right saying of my granny. That one about looking up at God and other things looking up too.

"Mother!" Sasha screams this so loud that I almost drop the not-smushed box of cupcakes.

Sasha runs to her mother and says, "You're late!" in a mean voice that would get me sent to my room to think about what I said.

I wait for Sasha's mommy to tell her to sit down and think about that voice. But she just looks at our clock on the wall. "No, I'm not, honey. I'm a few minutes early."

"But it's not fair!" Sasha whines. "Natalie already started *her* party. It's our turn now!"

Miss Hines whispers to Laurie and me, "Would you girls sit down for a little bit. We'll pass out cupcakes a little later. Okay?" She gets up from her desk and helps Sasha's mom with some of the sacks and boxes she's carrying. "Plenty of time for both parties. Thanks for coming."

Laurie and I sit back down. Without cupcakes.

Sasha's mom runs back to the car for another load of stuff. The principal of the whole entire school helps her carry things and then leaves real fast.

"Sasha, sweetheart, would you please give everyone a plate and a napkin for me?" her mom asks.

"We already got napkins!" Jason shouts.

"Not like *these* napkins," Sasha says.

I have to admit she's right about that. Sasha's napkins are so big they cover our whole desks. Plus, they are purple. Plus also, they have cats in birthday hats on them. And we each get a party hat just like that.

Sasha's mom walks up each desk lane and plops down the biggest cookie I've ever seen onto that napkin. It's a great cookie, with chocolate chips and chocolate frosting and more frosting inside of it. Plus purple candies that spell out SASHA on every cookie.

But cookies are not cupcakes. I think cupcakes are fancier than cookies. That's what.

"Shall we start the first game?" Sasha's mother asks. She writes in big letters on the blackboard: SASHA. Then under those letters she writes NATALIE. "Let's see how many words we can make out of the birthday girls' names."

"As!" Sasha shouts.

Her mother writes "AS" on the board under "SASHA."

"Has! Ash!" Sasha shouts.

Nobody else says anything. Finally, Anna says, "At?"

Sasha's mom writes "AT" under "NATALIE."

"I didn't know you were using her name too," Sasha says.

"Well, let's go on to the next game," Miss Hines says.

We play three more games that are more fun than words. Only not for me. Plus, there are prizes. And everybody ends up with a ball or a card game, even if they're losers. Like me.

"Is it time for cupcakes yet?" I ask my teacher.

"Good idea," Miss Hines answers. She holds out the box of not-smushed cupcakes.

Laurie and I hurry up for that box.

"*I* have cupcakes too!" Sasha shouts.

"You do?" Miss Hines says. "Well, okay then. Um . . . why don't we pass out all the cupcakes? Students, you can take whatever cupcake you want. Okay?"

I take the top off my cupcake box and hand the first cupcake to our teacher.

"It's lovely, Natalie," she says. She puts it on her fancy purple cat napkin.

Laurie and I start on the back row 'cause Sasha and her mom are on the front row. Anna takes one. "Thanks," she says.

Farah takes one. "These are very nice, Natalie," she says. "Thank you."

"Man! These are awesome!" Matthew, a front-row boy, hollers. "I never saw cupcakes like these! Cool! Mine has a real whistle on it." He blows the whistle.

"I have a fan on mine," Bethany says. "It really works."

"Who cares?" Griff says. "Look at the size of this cake!"

The back-row people get out of their seats to go look. Nobody else takes one of my cupcakes when Laurie and I walk by with our cupcake box. Anna

puts hers back. Farah doesn't. But she takes one of
Sasha's too.

I can't blame her. Even Laurie and I take one
of Sasha's cupcakes. They are the most gorgeous
purpley giant cupcakes I ever saw. Plus there are
prizes on top.

Everybody helps with cleanup. The school bell
rings. Party's over.

I walk out into the hall with two boxes full of
cupcakes. One smushed. One not chosen.

Then before I go outside, I dash into the
girls' bathroom. And I dump both boxes into the
wastebasket.

Chapter 15

Let's Party!

Saturday, I feel bad twitchy in my stomach. On account of I am having a birthday party, but nobody is coming.

Mommy is in the kitchen covering up my birthday cake so the germs don't get in. Daddy is in the family room dropping clothespins into jars. It's a game. Granny and I are waiting in the living room.

"Where is everybody?" Granny asks. She peeks out the front window for the gazillionth time.

"Laurie will be here. Laurie's mom made her go help pick up Laurie's sister Brianna. Brianna got to sleep over at a friend's. Only she was still sleeping over when they got there. And she is hard to hurry up." My bestest friend was crying on the phone when she told me this.

"But where's everybody else?" Granny demands. "You'd think they'd all come early just for the cake. Your mom told me how they ate every cupcake at your kindergarten party."

I look down at my foot. Not at Granny.

"What?" Granny quits staring out the window. She stares at me. "Nat? Come clean, girl."

I don't want to hurt Granny's feelings. "Maybe they didn't eat *all* the cupcakes," I admit.

Granny bends down lower so I have to see her. "Spill it, kid."

And I do. I've been holding the whole kindergarten party inside of me. Now it comes gushing out like a volcano cake. I tell Granny about Sasha and her mother. And the big cookies. And the games. And the napkins.

And the fancy cupcakes with prizes on top.

And how Sasha invited everybody to a better-than-mine party that lasts the whole day.

When I'm done, Granny says, "That just dills my pickle. That's what."

"I threw our cupcakes in the wastebasket." I didn't want to say this part. But saying it to Granny makes my stomach stop feeling so twitchy.

Granny hugs me. Hard. In a very good way.

The front door flies open. "I'm here!" Laurie shouts. "Sorry I'm late. Bri's fault. Boy, is she in trouble."

Granny hugs my bestest friend. "You're just in time, Laurie."

"Am I also in time?"

We all turn to the open door to see who said this. It's Farah. Standing behind her is a woman who looks like Farah, with big brown eyes and black

hair. "Is this the home of Farah's friend Natalie?" the woman asks.

"It certainly is," Granny says. She introduces herself and us to Farah's mom.

I take Farah's coat for her. "Thanks for coming, Farah."

"Did you get invited to Sasha's party?" Laurie asks.

"No," Farah admits. "But I would still come here if I had this other party invitation."

Laurie and I give each other smiley faces. Then we each take one of Farah's hands and go to the kitchen to meet Mommy.

As soon as Farah's mom leaves, Granny turns on music. "Let's party!" she shouts.

Daddy shows us how to drop clothespins into a jar.

We are in the middle of a game of Pass the Orange when Jason comes running into the family room.

"I love that orange game!" he shouts. "My turn!" It turns out he went to Sasha's party *and* my party. Only I know he missed a lot of great playing at Sasha's party. I am done being aggravated at my bestest friend who is a boy, Jason.

Just the kids sit at a little round table so I can open my presents. I get nail polish from Laurie. Plus there are stickers to put on top of the polish. I love nail polish. Farah and her mother made me a box out of tiny seashells. It is filled with beautifulness. Jason got me a baseball. And he signed it.

"Thanks for the presents, everybody," I say. "They're the best presents in the world." This feels like a true thing.

Mom cuts us giant pieces of cake.

"We gotta pray first," I say before Jason eats his whole cake. I take Farah's hand, and Laurie takes her other hand. I take Jason's hand. And we're all hand-holders around the table.

Then I talk to God, only out loud. "God, thanks for this super birthday party. And my really-and-for-true friends. And this cake filled with gorgeousness.

Plus I hope you got good birthday parties when you were a little boy. Like at Christmas."

"Can we eat yet?" Jason whispers.

"Amen," I say. I take a big bite of my cake. And guess what. It is the best cake in the world. That's what.

"How old is God?" Farah asks. She takes tiny cake bites.

"My sister Sarah says God's as far up as numbers go," Laurie answers.

"I do not understand," Farah says.

"Yeah. Me neither," Laurie admits.

"I think God is really, really, really, really old," I say. "Like twenty-four maybe? But he never looks a day older every time you see him."

I say a secret, to-myself, open-eyes prayer and thank God for my friends. And I thank him for being at my party, like he is at kindergarten, and church, and the HyKlas.

Anna shows up in time to play Red Rover. Plus two other kids come too.

We get seconds on everything 'cause there's lots of food and still not lots of people at my party. That makes me a tiny bit of sad. But not too much. On account of I really like the people who *are* here.

I don't have horse rides. Or jumping boxes. Or bowling. But at my house, we have each other.

And one more thing.

A really happy birthday! That's what.

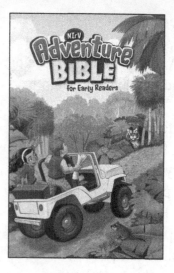

Adventure Bible for Early Readers, NIrV

Now kids 6-9 can share in the love for God's Word with *The Adventure Bible for Early Readers*. Based on the bestselling *Adventure Bible* and written in the New International Reader's Version (NIrV—"The NIV for Kids!"), this Bible is designed especially for early readers who are ready to explore the Bible on their own.

The Adventure Bible for NIrV: Book of Devotions for Early Readers

Buckle up, hold tight, and get ready for adventure! *The NIrV Adventure Bible Book of Devotions for Early Readers* takes kids on the ride of their lives. This yearlong devotional carries young children on a thrilling journey of spiritual growth and discovery.

Available now at your local bookstore!